George Brown, CLASS CLOWN
Lice Check

D0367139

For Amanda, for reasons only she will
understand—NK

For Deanna (finally), thanks for putting
up with all of us for so long!—AB

GROSSET & DUNLAP
Published by the Penguin Group
Penguin Group (USA) LLC, 375 Hudson Street, New York, New York 10014, USA

USA | Canada | UK | Ireland | Australia | New Zealand | India | South Africa | China

penguin.com
A Penguin Random House Company

Text copyright © 2014 by Nancy Krulik. Illustrations copyright © 2014 by Aaron Blecha.
All rights reserved. Published by Grosset & Dunlap, a division of Penguin Young Readers
Group, 345 Hudson Street, New York, New York 10014. GROSSET & DUNLAP is a
trademark of Penguin Group (USA) LLC. Printed in the USA.

Library of Congress Cataloging-in-Publication Data is available.

ISBN 978-0-448-46112-0   10 9 8 7 6 5 4 3 2

George Brown, CLASS CLOWN

Lice Check

by Nancy Krulik
illustrated by Aaron Blecha

Grosset & Dunlap
An Imprint of Penguin Group (USA) LLC

Chapter 1

"My head itches," George Brown said as he scratched hard at his scalp. "Bad."

"Mine, too," George's best friend Alex added. "I'm hoping it's psychosomatic."

"Psycho *what?*" George asked him.

"Psy-cho-so-mat-ic," Alex repeated slowly. He scratched the back of his neck. "It means it's all in your head."

"Which is where lice wind up," George said. **"On your head."**

"Not *on* your head," Alex explained. "*In* your head. When you hear someone say the word *lice* it makes you itch, **even if you don't have any**."

George sure hoped Alex was right and

he was just imagining the **itchy** feeling all over his head. The last thing he wanted was to be sent home with bugs in his hair.

"I hate lice checks," Julianna told George and Alex. "It always takes the nurse so long to go through my hair." She scratched her head.

Seeing Julianna scratch made George scratch. Which made Alex scratch. A lot of the kids waiting in the lice-check line were scratching. Sage was scratching so hard George thought she might make her scalp bleed.

The only kid not scratching was Louie Farley. "I'm not worried about having lice," Louie explained. "My brother, Sam, went through lice checks the whole time he was here, and he never once had them. **Lice know better than to invade a Farley forehead**."

"I guess brains know better than to invade a Farley forehead, too," George whispered to Alex.

Alex laughed as quietly as he could. "I'll say," he whispered. "No one is immune to a lice invasion—except maybe bald guys."

"I'd rather have lice than be bald," George said. He scratched the back of his ear.

This itching was awful. But not nearly as awful as the **bubbling feeling** George suddenly felt in the bottom of his belly.

Bing-bong. Ping-pang.

George gulped. Those bubbles weren't just your usual, run-of-the-mill kind of bubbles. They were strong, powerful bubbles. Bubbles that slam-danced against his spleen and kickboxed with his kidneys. Bubbles that could **burst out of him** at any moment, and . . .

4

B-U-U-U-R-P!

George let out a powerful burp. A **super burp**. A burp so loud and so strong, it knocked a louse right off the head of a fifth-grader waiting in line to be checked. And, boy, was that louse surprised.

"Dude, no!" Alex gulped.

Dude, yes! The burp had been set free. And now whatever the burp wanted to do, George would do.

The next thing George knew, he was on all fours, crawling all around the floor like **a wild, crazy giant louse**.

"George! Get back in line and wait for your lice check!" his teacher, Mrs. Kelly, scolded.

George wanted to get back in line to wait and not **bug** everyone. He really did. But he was powerless. The burp was in charge now. And it didn't feel like waiting in line like a good student. It felt like crawling around like a lousy louse.

So George crawled right down the lice-check line. Past Julianna. Past Sage. Past Max. Past Mike. He didn't stop crawling until he was right in front of Louie!

"Get away from me, you weirdo freak!" Louie shouted.

George's hand reached out and started tickling Louie's tummy—like a louse tickling someone's head. "Cut that out!" Louie complained. Then he started wiggling and jiggling, too. Only Louie wasn't wiggling because of a burp. Louie was wiggling because he was ticklish.

Tickle, tickle, tickle. George's fingers tickled Louie's armpits. George didn't want to be sticking his fingers in Louie's pits. But he couldn't help himself. *Tickle, tickle, tickle.*

"Cut . . . ha-ha-ha . . . it . . . ha-ha-ha . . . out!" Louie said.

But George kept tickling. *Tickle . . . tickle . . . tick . . . POP!* Just then George felt something burst in the bottom of his belly. All the air rushed out of him. The super burp was gone.

But George was still there. With **his fingers in Louie's pits**. Yuck.

"George Brown! Keep your hands to yourself," Mrs. Kelly told him.

George pulled his hands back. "I'm sorry," he said quietly. And he meant it. He was really sorry he had touched Louie's sweaty armpits. **Gross.**

Chapter 2

"I'm glad this day's over," George said as he sat down at the table in Alex's living room after school.

"Yeah. That was a bad burp," Alex said. "We gotta find you a cure before something really awful happens."

"Something really awful *did* happen," George insisted. "I can't believe I stuck my fingers in Louie's pits," he groaned. "I washed my hands three times, with soap, and they still **stink.**"

"I've never seen anything like your super burp," Alex said. "I've read all the scientific websites I could find, and I've never found documentation of a burp like that. Your

burps are real record breakers."

Usually being told he was a **record breaker** would have made George happy. Especially coming from Alex, who was the only kid he knew who had made it into the *Schminess Book of World Records*. But having a record-breaking burp did not make George happy.

It all started on George's first day at Edith B. Sugarman Elementary School. George's dad was in the army, and his family moved around a lot. So there always seemed to be some new school where he was the new kid.

But this time, George had promised himself that things were going to be **different**. He was turning over a new leaf. **No more pranks.** No more being the class clown. He wasn't going to get into trouble anymore, like he had at all his old schools. He was going to raise his hand before he spoke. He wasn't going to make funny faces or goof on his teachers behind their backs.

At the end of his first day, George had managed to stay out of trouble. But you didn't have to be a math whiz like Alex to figure out how many friends being a well-behaved, not-so-funny kid will get you. Zero. Zilch. *None.*

That night, George's parents took him out to Ernie's Ice Cream Emporium. While they were sitting outside and George was finishing his root beer float, **a shooting star flashed across the sky**. So George made a wish.

I want to make kids laugh—without getting into trouble.

Unfortunately, the star was gone before George could finish the wish. So only half came true—**the first half**.

A minute later, George had a funny feeling in his belly. It was like there were

13

hundreds of tiny bubbles bouncing around in there. The bubbles bounced up and down and all around. They ping-ponged their way into his chest, and bing-bonged their way up into his throat. And then . . .

George let out a big burp. A *huge* burp. A SUPER burp!

The super burp was loud, and it was *magic*.

Suddenly George lost control of his arms and legs. It was like they had minds of their own. His hands grabbed straws and stuck them up his nose like a walrus. His feet jumped up on the table and started dancing the **hokey pokey**. Everyone at Ernie's Emporium started laughing—except George's parents, who were covered in ice cream from the sundaes he had knocked over.

The magic super burp came back many times after that. And every time the burp came, it brought **trouble**. Like the time it made him act like a dog and start barking during the fourth-grade field day. He'd even **licked** Principal McKeon's hand! *Blech!*

George never knew when a burp would strike or what it would make him do. He might dive-bomb headfirst into Principal McKeon's lap during the school talent show. Or drop raw pizza dough on his head. Or literally dance his pants off on a live TV show. Millions of TV viewers had gotten a good view of George's **tighty whities** that time!

The only other person who knew about the super burp was Alex. Luckily, Alex was such a great friend that he was using all his scientific know-how to try to find a way to squelch that belch once and for all.

"Don't worry," Alex told George. "We'll find a burp cure. You'll see."

George looked at the floor. He didn't really feel like talking about the burp anymore. He'd rather talk about anything else. Even *lice*.

"I've never actually seen a louse up close," George told Alex. "Have you?"

Alex shook his head. Then he started to type something on his computer.

"Well, this is what they look like," Alex said. He moved away from the computer so George could see the video image of the top of some guy's head. There were bugs crawling around his part and white dots stuck to his hair.

"It says that the white things are nits," Alex told George. **"Lice eggs, waiting to hatch."**

"Whoa," George said. Some of the little white eggs were hatching. George **scratched** his scalp. "You better turn that off," he told Alex. "Just *looking* at those lice is making me itch."

George really hoped he didn't get any bugs or nits on his head. It was bad enough having a magical super burp around. He didn't need lice, too. How much trouble could one guy take?

Chapter 3

"How come you didn't come to school with Chris today?" Alex asked George as the boys headed into their classroom Friday morning. "You guys always walk together."

"Yeah," George said, "except when there are **bugs walking around on Chris's head**."

"Oh." Alex nodded. "Chris got lice, huh?"

"Yup," George told him. "A bunch of kids in his class had it. What's worse is Chris gave lice to his sister and brother. All three of them are home today. His mom's cleaning their whole house."

"Bummer," Louie said as he walked by and sat down at his desk. He let out a little laugh. It didn't sound like he felt bad for Chris **at all**.

George scowled. Louie could be a real jerk. But today he was a real *stinky* jerk. George pinched his nose and moved his desk away from Louie's. "You smell," he said.

"Yeah, what's with the garlic?" Alex asked.

Louie fingered the **necklace of garlic** he was wearing around his neck. "This will keep the lice away," he announced in a voice so loud, the whole class heard him.

Everyone turned and looked at Louie, which was exactly what Louie had been hoping for. Louie loved being the center of attention.

"Garlic wards off lice," Louie told the kids.

"That's for **vampires**," Julianna said. "Not lice."

Sage nodded. "Julianna's right. I saw it in a movie once."

"Well, actually, lice are sort of like vampire *bats*," Alex said. "Vampire bats bite into cattle and suck their blood. Lice dig their claws into human scalps and then suck the blood right out."

"That's what I told you guys," Louie said.

21

George laughed. That wasn't at all what Louie had said. He probably had no idea what lice ate. But Alex did. Alex knew all kinds of scientific stuff.

"Of course, there's no evidence that garlic keeps vampire bats *or* lice away," Alex continued.

"Boy, Alex," George said. "You're going to be an amazing scientist **when you grow up**."

"Thanks," Alex said with a smile.

"He could be a *mathemachicken*, too," Max pointed out. "He knows a lot of math."

"That's mathema*tician*," Louie corrected Max. "And I could be one of those, too. Did you see how fast I did the long-division problem at the board yesterday?"

"That was really amazing," Max said. He gave Louie a big smile.

George rolled his eyes. It wasn't that amazing. Louie hadn't even gotten the problem right.

Mrs. Kelly stopped writing on the board and turned to smile at the class. "I'm so glad to hear you all discussing different **careers**," she said.

George looked at Mrs. Kelly **strangely**. They hadn't really been talking about careers. They were mostly talking about vampires, bats, and blood. Cool stuff. But leave it to a teacher to find the lesson in anything.

"After all," Mrs. Kelly continued, "as you know, Career Day is coming up next Tuesday. So the more you think about what careers you want to learn about, the better. Becoming a mathematician or a scientist are both really great career options. But there's no reason to decide now what profession you will have when you grow up. Not with so many to choose from."

Mrs. Kelly gave the kids one of her gummy smiles. George could see a big piece of **yellow goo** on one of her teeth. Apparently, Mrs. Kelly had eggs for breakfast.

"I am very pleased that so many of your parents have agreed to come to school on Tuesday to talk to all the fourth- and fifth-graders about their careers," Mrs. Kelly continued. "The whole gym will be filled with Career Day booths. You can walk around and see lots of presentations."

"Do we have to go around to all the booths?" Max asked.

"You couldn't possibly see them all. There will be too many," Mrs. Kelly answered. "So you should pick the ones that seem the most interesting to you."

"Since we won't have any classes on Tuesday, does that mean **no homework** Monday night?" Mike wondered.

"Well, actually, you will each have a report to hand in Tuesday morning *before* you go into the gym," Mrs. Kelly told him. "I want you to interview one of your parents about his or her career."

"I already know all about my dad's career," Louie said. "He's a lawyer. He sues people."

"I'm sure there's a lot more to it than that," Mrs. Kelly said.

"Oh yeah," Louie agreed. "It's hard work being a lawyer. My dad is exhausted from it. He comes home and collapses on the couch every night. You should hear him **snoring**."

George rolled his eyes. Louie didn't make being a lawyer sound like much fun. Not that that was too surprising, coming from Louie. George figured Louie might grow up to be a vampire one day. He already knew how to **suck the fun out of everything**— even something as cool as Career Day.

Chapter 4

Grumble. Rumble.

George was so hungry that his stomach seemed to be talking to him. *Feed me. Feed me,* it grumbled. But his stomach was going to have to wait.

"I can't believe we're having another lice check. And *before* lunch," George complained. He scratched his itchy head and patted his empty stomach. "I wish Nurse Cuttaway would hurry up. I'm **starving**."

"I think it's taking her so long because so many kids have lice today," Alex told him. "Look over in the Lice Corner."

The Lice Corner was the part of the

hall where the kids who had lice were forced to sit until their parents came and got them. There were twenty kids sitting there—and Nurse Cuttaway had only gone through about half of the school's heads.

George scratched his scalp again. He swore he **felt something crawling around** up there. He hoped he was just imagining it.

"No! I can't! It can't be true!"

George suddenly heard someone scream. He looked over at the lice chair and saw Sage. She was holding her hands over her face and **sobbing**.

"I'm sorry, Sage," Nurse Cuttaway told her. "But you'll have to go home and wash your hair with Louse-Away shampoo."

"I can't have lice. I can't!" Sage cried. She suddenly leaped up from the chair and started running down the hall. She stopped when she reached George. "*Georgie*, help me," she sobbed.

Oh man. George hated when Sage called him Georgie. It was so embarrassing. What did Sage want him to do about this, anyway?

Sage stopped crying long enough to flutter her eyelashes. "I need a hug."

Oh no. No way was that happening. George wouldn't hug Sage on a good day—never mind a day when she had lice crawling around on her head. He had to get away from her.

"I'll go next," George volunteered, pushing his way to the front of the lice-check line.

George plopped himself down in Nurse Cuttaway's chair and folded his arms. There. Sage couldn't get him here. No one with lice was allowed near the lice-check station. They had to stay put in the Lice Corner.

Which meant George was safe as long as he was in this chair.

Squeak, squeak, squeak. Nurse Cuttaway's rubber-gloved hands rubbed at his scalp. But George didn't care. Not this

time. Those rubber gloves were saving
him from hugging a lice-covered Sage! As
far as George was concerned, they were
heroes!

"I'm so excited for Career Day," Alex
said as he set his lunch tray down next to
George in the cafeteria a little while later.
"My mom's coming to share what it's like
to be a dentist. She loves talking to kids
about healthy teeth."

"I asked my dad to come instead of my mom," George said. "Everyone in school has been to my mom's craft store, so they already know about her job. But I doubt anyone has been on the army base where my dad works." He opened his milk container and took a big swig. "Everyone's going to want to hear about that. **My dad's booth is going to be mobbed**."

"I wouldn't bet on it," Louie interrupted as he sat down at the table across from Alex and George. Mike and Max took seats on either side of him.

"Why not?" George asked Louie. "Don't you think being in the army is interesting?"

"Maybe," Louie replied with a shrug. "But not as interesting as being a lawyer. And there won't be any kids at your dad's booth, because everyone is going to be busy listening to *my* dad."

"Yeah, everybody," Max told George.

"Every single kid," Mike added. Then he stopped and looked at Louie. "But then there won't be any kids coming by to hear my dad talk about what it's like to be a mailman."

"Sure there will," Louie said. "When my dad's booth gets too crowded, I'll send the overflow to your dad's booth."

"Oh. Okay. Cool," Mike said.

"It can't be that interesting being a lawyer," George grumbled.

"You wanna bet?" Louie asked menacingly.

George gulped. When Louie sounded like that, he was usually pretty sure of himself. For some reason, he was certain his dad was going to be the most popular guy at Career Day. And he must be sure he could use that fact to make a **fool** out of George. Making George look like a fool was Louie's favorite hobby.

Still, there was no way George was going to let Louie claim that his dad was better than George's dad. No way at all.

"Yeah. **I do want to bet**," George said defiantly. "I bet you my dad will have more kids coming to his booth than your dad will." He held out his hand to shake on it.

But Louie didn't shake. Instead he said, "If you want to bet, then we should make this more **interesting**."

"Definitely," Mike agreed.

"Yeah, interesting," Max added. Then he looked at Louie. "Actually a bet is already kind of interesting."

"And a bet for something is even more interesting," Louie said. He smiled at George. "Tell you what. If more people come to see my dad at the fair than come to see yours, you have to give me that skeleton ring you're always flashing around."

George gulped. **His skeleton ring?** The one with the red stones for eyes? The one George had bought with the money that he'd earned working at Mr. Furstman's pet store?

George loved that ring. He really did. But he wasn't going to back down. Not from Louie. He was going to

defend his dad. Like a good soldier. Well, a good soldier's *son*, anyway.

"Okay," George said slowly. "And if more people show up to my dad's booth, then . . ." George paused for a minute. What did Louie have that George would really want? It was hard to decide. Louie had everything. But the one thing he had that George *really* wanted was . . .

"You have to give me your sneakers with wheels in them!" George shouted suddenly.

"My wheelie sneakers?" Louie **gulped**. "My mom would kill me if I gave those away."

"That's the bet," George said. **"Take it or leave it."**

Louie took a deep breath. "Okay," he said finally. Then he smiled. "It's no big deal, anyway. **I'm not gonna lose.**"

"Me neither," George said, trying to sound confident. He twirled his skeleton ring around on his finger. At least he hoped he wouldn't.

"How are you guys going to keep track of how many kids actually show up at your dads' booths?" Alex asked George and Louie.

George thought about that for a minute. "I know," he said finally. "We'll have sign-in sheets at our booths."

"Yeah," Louie agreed. "And the guy with **the most signatures** of people who showed up wins."

"Great idea, Louie," Max said.

"You're so smart, Louie," Mike added.

George rolled his eyes. The sign-in sheets hadn't been Louie's idea. But there was no point in reminding Max and Mike about that.

"Okay, now that that's settled, I'm gonna eat my lunch," Louie said. He opened his lunch bag and took out his turkey sandwich. Then he unwrapped a thin package of **red powder** and poured it on top of his turkey.

"What's that?" Max asked Louie.

"Chili powder," Louie told him.

"That's **hot** stuff," Alex said. "You sure you want to use all of it?"

"I'm sure," Louie replied. "The hotter the better, if I want to keep the lice away."

"What are you talking about?" Max asked him.

"Hey, I was gonna ask him that!" Mike said.

"Well, *I* asked first," Max told Mike.

George choked back a laugh. These guys were ridiculous.

"Don't worry, I'll tell you both," Louie said. "I'm gonna eat something spicy so my temperature will go up, and any louse that might be near me will **burn up** on contact."

"It doesn't work that way," Alex told Louie.

"Sure it does," Louie said. "When you eat spicy foods, you sweat. You sweat when you get hot. And heat burns things."

Alex shook his head. "Even if your internal temperature goes up enough to make you sweat, it's only for an instant. And it isn't hot enough to actually burn something on the outside of your body."

"You don't know everything," Louie told Alex. And with that, he took a big bite of his turkey-and-chili-powder sandwich.

For a minute, Louie just sat there, chewing. And then, suddenly, **his face turned beet red**. His mouth opened and his tongue dropped out.

"AAAAHHHHH!" Louie shouted. He poured his juice box down his throat in one gulp. Then he grabbed Max's water and drank that, too. Finally he grabbed Mike's juice. But the box was **empty**.

"Sorry, Louie," Mike said. "I drank it already."

Louie didn't hear Mike's apology. He'd already jumped up from the table and was **racing toward the water fountain** at the other side of the cafeteria.

George decided right then and there that he was officially a big fan of chili powder. He didn't know if it could get rid of lice. But it had gotten rid of Louie. And getting rid of Louie was *always* a good thing.

46

Chapter 5

"Are you worried about losing your ring to Louie?" Alex asked George late Saturday afternoon. The boys were visiting the army base with George's dad, so George could do some research for the paper he had to turn in on Tuesday.

"A little," George admitted. "I mean I know being in the army has to be more interesting than being a lawyer, but Louie sure sounded confident."

"Louie always sounds confident," Alex reminded George. "Even when he's wrong. **And he's wrong a lot.**"

George smiled. Alex was trying to make him feel better. And it worked, at least a little. But George was still worried that Louie had some **trick up his sleeve** to help him win the ring right off George's finger.

"Come on, boys, hurry up," George's dad said. "We're going to be late for chow."

George picked up his pace. "Chow" meant food. Which was good, because George was plenty hungry.

"Hey, Sarge, is this your boy?" one of the soldiers working behind the food counter asked as George and Alex took their places in line.

George grinned. He loved it when people called his dad "Sarge."

"Yes, this is George," his dad said. "And this is his best friend, Alex. They're here to study what goes on at an army base."

The soldier behind the counter placed a plate on George's tray. George looked down. Roast chicken, mashed potatoes, and cooked spinach. Not bad—except for the **spinach**.

George hated spinach. It always felt like pieces of **slimy green skin** sliding down his throat.

"Okay, boys," George's dad said as they sat down at a table in the mess hall. "Eat up. And don't take too long. There's a lot to see around here. An army base is a really cool place."

George was counting on that. He had

to get lots of other kids to come learn
about his dad's army career, so he could
get to keep his ring—and earn himself a
new pair of wheelie sneakers, too!

"These are the barracks," George's
dad said a little while later, as the boys
walked into a room where some of the
soldiers on the base lived.

George looked around. It seemed as though they were in a small apartment. In fact, if it weren't called a barracks, there would be **nothing special** about this place at all. It was just a place to live—with a bathroom, a bedroom, and a small kitchen.

George fingered his skeleton ring nervously. If things didn't get more interesting around the base, he wouldn't have the ring much longer.

"Um . . . Dad . . . is there anything **really cool** going on around here?" he

asked his father. "I mean something [could talk about with the kids at school.

"Sure," George's dad assured him. "We've only just begun our tour. Come on."

The boys followed as George's dad led them back outside. There were soldiers all over the base. Going in and out of buildings. Standing around, chatting with each other. Talking on cell phones.

"This is **boring**," George whispered to Alex. "And that's *baaaddd*."

"Maybe it will get better." Alex looked around the base.

Suddenly a smile formed on his face. "Check out those soldiers," he said, pointing to an obstacle course.

George looked over and saw a group of soldiers **climbing up the side of a tower**, while another group rappelled down the other side on ropes. "Why are they doing that?" he wondered aloud.

"It helps make them better soldiers," George's dad explained.

Alex looked up at George's dad. "How does going up

and down a tower do that?"

"The obstacle course builds confidence," George's dad answered. "And it makes sure the soldiers stay **in shape**."

"We do stuff like that in gym," George said. "Only we don't climb up so high."

"And we don't **slither in the mud** or crawl under nets," Alex added, pointing at some soldiers who were further along in the course. He turned to George. "That's kind of cool."

George didn't answer. He just stood there watching the soldiers climb up and go down the wall, and slither in the mud. It looked fun.

But was it more fun than being a lawyer? George had no idea, because he didn't really know what lawyers did.

The only thing George knew for sure was that there was trouble brewing on the army base. He knew that because it was brewing in the bottom of his belly. And it was the kind of enemy even the US Army couldn't stop. **The super burp was back.**

Bling-blonk. Pling-plonk. The bubbles were using George's insides as an obstacle course. Already they had slithered up George's side, and maneuvered their way through his middle. Now they were trekking up through his trachea.

George tried to signal Alex for help, but there wasn't time.

B·U·U·U·R·P!

George let out a super burp **so loud** the soldiers at the top of the tower could hear it.

"Did you say something, Sarge?" one of the men called down.

George opened his mouth to say, "Excuse me," but that's not what came out. Instead, he started counting. "Hup, two, three, four. Hup, two, three, four."

Then George's legs started marching. "Hup, two, three, four. Hup, two, three, four."

"George, where do you think you're going?" his father asked him.

George didn't answer. He couldn't. **He had no idea** where he was going. The burp hadn't told him yet.

But a minute later, the burp let George know exactly what he was in for. The burp was in the mood to try the army obstacle course. So the next thing George knew, he was climbing one of the long ropes, heading for the top of the tower.

George's arms pulled him higher and higher up the rope. He didn't dare **look down**. He was too far off the ground. George didn't like being up there at all. But the burp didn't mind. Burps aren't afraid of heights.

"George! Get down from there!" his father shouted.

"You're acting like a wild animal!"

Boy, did George wish he could listen to his dad. But he couldn't. The burp was going wild. So George was going wild.

Suddenly, George felt the rope start swinging back and forth.

"A-ha-ha-ha-ha-ha!" George's mouth let out a loud yell as his body swung back and forth on the rope. **"Me Tarzan!** A-ha-ha-ha-ha-ha!"

"Oh, this is bad," Alex muttered. George's hands let go of the rope and banged at his chest like Tarzan.

"A-ha-ha . . . WHOA!" he shouted as he fell straight down onto the mesh net stretched out below him.

A bunch of soldiers were crawling under the net on their bellies. George flipped and flopped as the soldiers crept beneath him. He looked like **a fish** caught in a net. *Flip. Flop. Flip.*

"George, get over here!" his father shouted up to him. "That's an order!"

Ordinarily, George would never ignore a direct order from his dad. But George wasn't in charge right now. The super burp was. And burps don't take orders from anyone. Not even sergeants in the US Army!

George's arms and legs scrambled off the net. He started running toward the tall tower. And **the next thing he knew**, George was climbing the tower alongside the soldiers. Higher and higher he climbed. And then . . .

POP! George felt something burst in his belly. All the air rushed out of him. It was as though someone had popped a balloon inside of him. The magical super burp was gone.

But George was still there, on the side of the tower. He looked down and **gulped**.

The ground was very far away. George opened his mouth to yell, "HELP!" And that's exactly what came out.

"I gotcha, kid," one of the soldiers said. He grabbed George around the middle, carried him down from the tower, and hurried him over to where George's dad was standing.

"Th-thanks," George **stammered** as the soldier placed him back on solid ground and saluted.

George's dad saluted back. "Thank you, Private," he told him.

"You're welcome, sir," the private said.

"George, what were you thinking?" his father asked him. "You could have been killed up there. **I don't understand what gets into you sometimes.**"

George didn't answer. He knew the truth. It wasn't what got into him. It was what burst out of him. *Stupid burp.* It was always getting him in trouble.

"I'm sorry," George told his dad.

"Not yet you aren't," George's dad insisted angrily. "But you will be, later. Come with me, boys."

"Wow!" George gasped as his dad led them into a giant room. He'd forgotten all about the obstacle course. It was hard to think about ropes and nets, or even burps, when you were standing right in front of a **giant helicopter**.

"I've never seen one of these up close," Alex said.

George looked up at the propellers. They were massive. Now this was **impressive**.

"Do you think this helicopter is too big to fit in the school gym?" he asked his dad.

George's dad laughed. "Yeah, I think it might be," he said. "But I can bring pictures of helicopters to Career Day."

George frowned. Pictures of army helicopters weren't nearly as cool as the real thing.

Just then, a soldier whose uniform had the same sergeant stripes as George's dad's walked over to where the boys were standing. "Are these my next passengers?" she asked George's dad.

Alex's eyes popped wide open. "Are you kidding?" he asked. "Yes, please, pick me!"

"Your mom signed a permission slip

for this yesterday," George's dad said with a grin. "We kept it a surprise."

A huge smile broke out across George's face. He wasn't thinking about his bet with Louie now. All he could think about was the fact that he and Alex were going to be up in the air in **a real live US Army helicopter**.

That's probably the coolest thing that could ever happen to a kid. He couldn't wait to be up there in the sky, looking down at all of Beaver Brook. He was so happy he felt like he could burst.

"Did you sign my permission slip, Dad?" George asked his father.

George's dad looked down at him and shook his head. "I did. But I've **changed my mind**. After what you did at the obstacle course, you're not going for a helicopter ride. I've got another army experience for you. It's something you're never going to forget."

Chapter 6

"You're sure you're not angry that I got to go for a ride in the helicopter and you didn't?" Alex asked George the next day as the boys walked up the path toward Alex's mom's dental office.

George shook his head. "Nope. It wasn't your fault the burp decided to show up."

"That punishment your dad gave you was **really harsh**," Alex said. "I can't believe how long it took you to clean those latrines."

"Well, it would have gone faster if I could have used a sponge instead of a toothbrush," George grumbled. "It was gross **cleaning toilets** with those teeny, tiny bristles."

"Your dad said it was an old army punishment," Alex said.

"I just hope my dad doesn't talk about cleaning toilets at Career Day," George said. He twisted his ring nervously. "How boring would that be? Kids would run out of his booth to Louie's dad's booth as fast as they could."

"If there are even any kids at school on Tuesday," Alex said. "My mom told me three of her patients canceled their weekend appointments because they had lice. I'm telling you, we're having **a bug epidemic** at school!"

George scratched his head. His mom had checked him for lice just that morning, so he knew he was still clean, but even thinking about the little bugs made him scratch.

"Oh yeah, I almost forgot," Alex said as he reached into his backpack and pulled out a thermos. "Before we go in there, you should drink this."

"Is that supposed to keep lice away?" George asked.

Alex shook his head. "Nope. **It keeps burps away.** It's lemon juice."

George looked at him strangely. Then he smiled. "Lemonade? Really? That's all it takes? Awesome. I love lemonade."

"It's actually not lemon*ade*," Alex explained. "It's lemon *juice*. Pure lemon juice. No extra water. No sugar. Just the sour stuff."

George made a face. That didn't sound very delicious.

"Lemons are filled with acid, so they stop your stomach from making any acid of its own," Alex explained. "No extra acid means no extra gas. **No gas means no bubbles, and that means no burps.**"

"Where'd you learn that?" George asked him.

"A woman posted all about it on the Burp No More Blog," Alex said. "She said this burp cure was foolproof. I figured today would be the best day to try it. I mean, yesterday at the army base was bad enough. But my mom . . ." Alex's voice trailed off.

George didn't blame Alex for being

worried that the burp would escape at his mom's dental office. Alex's mom had seen the burp make him do some really crazy things—like **skateboard on a beverage cart in an airplane** and crawl up into an overhead luggage bin.

Of course, that hadn't been George's fault. But Alex's mom didn't know that. So if drinking pure lemon juice meant he wouldn't cause any trouble at his best friend's mom's office, then George would do it.

Gulp. Gulp. Gulp. George drank down the lemon juice as fast as he could. His mouth filled with spit as the super-sour juice oozed down his throat. His **lips puckered** and his cheeks sucked themselves in against his teeth.

Alex laughed. "You look like a fish," he said. "Sorry it tastes so **nasty**. But it'll be worth it if it works. And I think it really might. Lemon juice is strong stuff."

George nodded. He only hoped it was strong enough.

"Good morning, boys," Alex's mom said as she led them into her examination room. She gave George a funny look. **"What's wrong with your face?"** she asked him.

"Too much lemon juice," George answered. A little bit of spit flew out of his mouth.

"Why would you drink that?" Alex's mom wondered.

George didn't answer. He wasn't sure what to say.

"Um . . . George just likes sour stuff," Alex answered for him.

Alex's mom shrugged and led the boys inside. "This is the examination room," she said. Then she added, "Please don't touch anything."

George knew that last part was for him. Alex's mom wanted to make sure that George didn't go **all wacko** and break something. George wanted to make sure of the same thing. Why else would he drink all that super-sour lemon juice?

"Check those out!" Alex said. He pointed to two tooth X-rays resting on a light box.

George glanced over at the X-rays. "Those look like **tree roots**," he said, pointing to the three long, skinny sticklike things that seemed to be growing out of the tooth. "Except they're growing up instead of down."

"Very good, George," Alex's mom said. "That's what we call them—roots."

Wow. George was relieved. For the first time in a long time, Alex's mom was smiling at him. And he didn't feel one bubble in his belly. So far, so good.

"Now, which of you boys would like to have your teeth cleaned first?" Alex's mom asked as she pulled out a tray of dental tools.

***Wait?* What? George gulped.** This wasn't supposed to be a trip to the dentist to . . . well . . . do dentist stuff. They were only supposed to be here so Alex could get information for his paper. George didn't want Alex's mom poking around in his mouth. Not today. Dental appointments weren't something George liked to have **sprung on him**.

"Um . . . Alex, you go first," George said. "That way you can write about what it feels like to be at the dentist."

"That's okay," Alex said. "Mom's always poking around in my mouth. You have the cleaning. I'll watch and take notes."

"That's a great idea!" Alex's mom said. "Come on, George. Hop up into the chair."

There was no getting out of it now. So George did the only thing he could do: He hopped up into the chair.

Alex's mom used a pedal on the floor to raise the chair higher so she could get a better look into George's mouth. Then she shined a bright light down his throat.

"Okay, now I'm going to just check

your teeth with my mirror and this little tool," Alex's mom said. "I'm going to need a little suction."

Alex's mom stuck a tube into his mouth. *Slurp*. The tube **sucked all the spit** out of George's mouth.

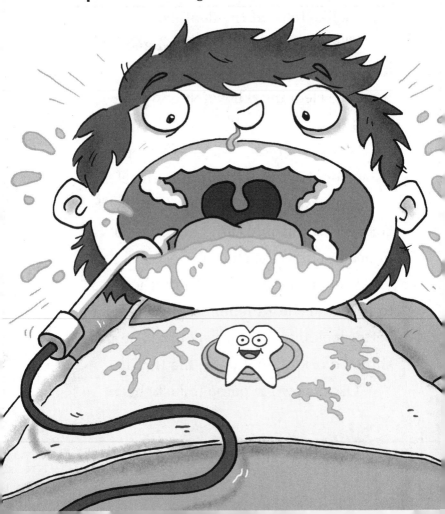

Alex's mom began to poke around at each of George's teeth. "Are you flossing every night?" she asked him.

George didn't answer. He couldn't. Not with a mirror, a dental pick, and a suction tube clogging up his mouth.

"Flossing is important," Alex's mom continued, "because plaque and tartar . . ."

Alex's mom kept talking, but George wasn't concentrating on what she was saying. All he could concentrate on was this **strange feeling** he had. Something was bouncing around inside his belly. Something bubbly. Something gassy.

Something like a *magic super burp*!

Oh no! Not here. Not now. George had to get out of here, before the burp got out of him!

Frantically, George **rubbed his head and tapped on his belly**. It was the secret signal he and Alex had for when the burp showed up. Whenever George gave the signal, Alex was supposed to help him get somewhere else so the burp wouldn't cause trouble. And if ever George needed to go somewhere else, it was now!

But Alex was too busy taking notes in his binder to see George rubbing and tapping.

"George, please sit still," Alex's mom said. "It's hard to scrape away plaque while you're **wiggling around**."

Sit still? How could George sit still? The *super burp* wasn't sitting still. Already it was rattling his ribcage and trampling over his tongue.

George couldn't even close his mouth, because Alex's mom had her hands in there. Which meant the bubbles twisting and turning their way around his teeth had a clear path right out of his . . .

BUUURP!

George let out a burp. **A mega burp.** A burp so loud and so huge you could hear it over a dentist's drill.

Uh-oh! The burp was on the loose! Which meant George was on the loose, too. No one could stop him.

"George, don't you usually say 'excuse me' after a burp like that?" Alex's mom asked.

George wanted to use his mouth to say excuse me. **He really did.** But George wasn't in charge any more. The burp was. So instead of apologizing, George's mouth spit the spit-sucking tube right into Alex's mom's face.

"Oh my!" Alex's mom shouted. "George, why did you do that?"

George had no idea why he had just done that. Because *he* hadn't done that. **The super burp had.** The same way the super burp was now making George jump out of the dentist's chair.

"Dude! Don't!" Alex shouted.

But magic super burps don't *don't*. Magic super burps *do*. And what this burp wanted to do was play with all the cool stuff in the dentist's office!

George's hands grabbed a toothbrush from a shelf.

"George, will you please calm down?" Alex's mom scolded.

No way! Magic super burps are never calm. And they are never down. They keep their energy waaayyyy up. George's hands reached toward Alex's mom.

"What are you . . ." Alex's mom started. But she didn't get to finish her sentence, because just then George's hands **shoved the toothbrush** into her open mouth.

"Brush, brush, brush!" George's mouth shouted. He moved the toothbrush up and down and up and down. "First your uppers. Then the ones down below. And don't forget to scrub the tongue."

Alex's mom yanked the toothbrush out of her mouth. "**Stop that!** I'm the dentist. I'm the only one allowed to put her hands in someone else's mouth."

George hurried over to the spit sink

next to the dental chair. "You want to rinse?" he asked Alex's mom.

"Dude, no!" Alex shouted nervously. "Keep away from the water."

Too late! George's hands were already on the little squirty thing in the sink. They turned on the faucet. George held the squirter up in the air. Water began flying all over the office. He looked like **a George fountain**.

POP! And then, suddenly, George felt all the air rush right out of him. It was like someone had popped a balloon in the bottom of his belly. **The super burp was gone.**

But George was still there. With water squirting all over him.

He opened his mouth to say, "I'm sorry." And that's exactly what came out.

"We'd better go," Alex said, quickly pushing George out the door. "I have plenty of stuff for my report."

"Oh no you don't!" Alex's mom said, stopping the boys in their tracks. "George isn't going anywhere until he cleans up this mess."

George frowned. He knew that was coming. Not that he blamed Alex's mom. There was water everywhere. And even though it wasn't really his fault, it sure seemed like it was.

"Okay," George said. "Where do you keep the sponges?"

Alex's mom shook her head. "You're not using a sponge," she told him as she walked over to a nearby shelf and picked up a toothbrush. **"You're using this to scrub up the mess.** And you'd better get started. Because with a toothbrush this small, it could take you all day."

George frowned. He was getting really sick of toothbrushes. Almost as sick as he was of magical super burps.

BONK!

Chapter 7

"Dude! You're back!" Alex cheered as Chris walked into the school yard with George on Monday morning.

"Yeah. I'm lice-free," Chris said. "It was such a hassle. I had to sit there for what seemed like an hour while some lady **picked through my hair** looking for lice nits."

"That's a career I never want to have," George said. "Nitpicker."

"That lady is getting a lot of business these days," Chris said. "Half the school has lice."

"Hi, *Georgie!*"

George gulped. Even without turning

around, he knew who was calling him. Sage was back!

"Did you miss me?" she asked, coming up beside George. "I missed you."

Oh brother. "A lot of people were out with lice," George told her. "It was hard to miss everyone."

"I had lice, too," Chris told Sage. "Did you have to wash your hair with that really **smelly shampoo**?"

"Uh-huh." Sage nodded. "My mom had to wash everything in my room in hot water, and she bagged up my stuffed animals for a whole week. She wasn't happy."

"Julianna got lice over the weekend," Alex said. "I talked to her last night. She went to the baseball center yesterday to do some batting practice and **came home scratching**. I bet she got lice from one of the helmets they make kids wear to protect their heads from being hit."

"Too bad they don't protect them from lice," Chris said.

"I hope Julianna gets back in time for Career Day tomorrow," George said. "I need all my friends here to go to my dad's booth."

"It looks like a lot of kids are absent today," Alex said, looking around the school yard. "I wonder if they're going to have to **cancel Career Day**. You may not have to worry about that bet after all, George."

George opened his mouth to say something, but before he could, Louie came **rolling over** on his wheelie sneakers.

"I figured you'd be really worried by now," Louie said. He looked down at George's hand. "You better polish that thing up really well tonight. I like wearing shiny jewelry."

"I'm not worried about anything," George insisted. "My dad's going to make his career sound really interesting. Kids will want to hear about it. And they'll come to his booth. I mean, if there are even any kids here tomorrow."

"Oh, there will be," Louie told him. "Even if it's just a few kids. That won't matter. As long as more of the kids who are there come to hear my dad talk than hear yours. I spent Saturday at my dad's office learning about lawyer stuff. His job is *very* interesting."

"As interesting as riding in **a helicopter**?" Alex asked Louie. "Because that's what I did when George and I visited the army base."

George didn't say anything about cleaning the latrines with a toothbrush. He didn't mention cleaning a dental office with a toothbrush, either. Instead he smiled at Louie. "Yeah," he said. "Helicopters are way cooler than desks. You better tie those shoelaces. I don't want you tripping and scratching the leather on my soon-to-be new wheelie sneakers!"

Louie frowned. That helicopter thing had obviously made him **nervous**. But he was trying really hard not to sound that way. "A helicopter's not such a big thing," he said. "It's not like your dad owns his own helicopter. You should see the giant desk my dad has in his office. It's his own. He doesn't share it with anyone. And it's huge! I got to sit behind my dad's desk. I saw his big, heavy, expensive law books. He has, like, a million of them. And we talked about how you go to court and sue people."

George smiled brighter and looked down at Louie's wheelie sneakers. Louie sounded **kind of nervous**. Those just might become George's sneakers after all.

Brrrriiinnnng. The school bell rang. It was time to go to class. Alex, Chris, and George headed toward the school building. Sage hurried to catch up to them.

Mike and Louie were walking into the building, too. George could hear them talking behind him.

"Listen, I need you to make sure

my dad gets a lot of kids to come to his booth," Louie told Mike. **"I don't care what you do to get them there."**

"But I'm supposed to be telling people to go to *my* dad's booth," Mike said.

"I thought you were my friend," Louie snarled.

"Oh, I am," Mike said. "Your best friend. I mean, look, I'm here with you today and Max isn't."

"Max has lice," Louie reminded him.

"Yeah, but I didn't get lice on purpose, just so I could be here with you, Louie," Mike insisted.

That was **the most ridiculous thing** George had ever heard. But he wasn't *supposed* to have heard it. So he didn't say a word. He just kept listening.

"I'll pay you to help me," Louie told Mike. "A quarter for every person you get into that booth. That could add up to a lot of moola! And kids can visit your dad's booth *after* they visit my dad's."

"You can count on me," Mike said finally. "I'll get you tons of kids. I'll have to, because Max isn't here to help." He sounded really proud to be Louie's only buddy at school.

"Don't worry," Louie said. "I'm gonna get Max to call all the other kids who are home with lice to make sure they get their heads cleaned up by tomorrow so they can visit my dad's booth."

George gulped. That wasn't fair. Louie was hiring his friends to help him win the bet. He opened his mouth to yell at Louie and Mike. But then he stopped himself. He didn't want Louie to know he'd been **eavesdropping**. And besides, Louie would just deny everything and say George had heard him wrong.

George was going to have to work even harder now to get kids to his dad's booth. Only there was no way he was going to cheat. The new-and-improved George didn't cheat. And he wouldn't ask his friends to cheat, either.

George was going to win this bet **fair and square**. But it wasn't going to be easy to do when he was up against a jerk like Louie.

Chapter 8

"I'm really glad I got back to school in time for this," Julianna said as she, George, Chris, and Alex walked into the gym on Tuesday morning. "Career Day looks amazing."

"Yeah," George agreed. He looked out at the rows of booths that lined the gym. "If it weren't for the basketball hoops, you'd never know this was the same place we played crab soccer. I wonder how they got rid of that **stinky gym-sock smell**."

"My mom's booth is over by the locker room," Alex said. "It still kind of smells there. Where'd they put your dad?"

"Under the basketball hoop, down at

the other end," George replied. "The booth's set up so kids get to go through an obstacle course. Then he shows them a video about US soldiers stationed **all over the world** helping people. He's even got a model tank and a model helicopter kids can look at."

"I'm definitely going to stop by your dad's booth after I visit my dad's architect station," Chris said. "He's showing kids how bridges are built."

"I'll be at your dad's booth," Julianna assured George. "Right after I help my parents demonstrate how to play the Yoruba triple drum they brought back from their trip to Africa."

"What do your parents do?" George asked Julianna. "All I know is that they're away a lot and your grandma stays with you."

"They're anthropologists," Julianna said. "They go all over the world and study

how people live. Wait until you see the
Mahākāla mask they brought home
from the Himalayan mountains. It's got
bloodred eyes and it's really spooky."

Just then, Mike walked over to where George and his friends were standing. "I'm going over to Louie's dad's booth," he told them. "I'll get to learn all about law and eat chocolate."

"Chocolate?" Chris asked. "What does that have to do with law?"

"Mr. Farley keeps a jar of candy on his big desk," Mike said. "So Louie brought candy to school. You guys should stop by."

George gave Mike a look. "Are you kidding? Do you really think *I'm* going to sign in at Louie's dad's booth?"

Mike shrugged. "Louie said to come over here. So I came over here."

As Mike walked away, George nervously fingered his ring. "No way can my dad beat free chocolate," he said. "Everyone's going to stop by Mr. Farley's booth. **Stick a fork in me. I'm done.**"

"There are plenty of kids at your dad's booth already," Julianna said. "Look."

George turned toward his dad's booth. There were kids jumping over orange cones and **wiggling on their bellies** under nets. They looked like they were having fun.

"Come on," Alex said. "Let's go do the obstacle course at your dad's booth."

"Okay," George agreed. He didn't say anything about visiting Alex's mom's booth. He figured she probably didn't want to see him for a while after what had happened in her office. Besides, George didn't want to see any more toothbrushes for a while—maybe in a bit, but not now. He hadn't even brushed his teeth this morning. He just ate a mint so he didn't have **stinky morning breath**.

George turned and looked around the gym. Louie was standing right out in front of his dad's booth, handing out lots and lots of chocolate bars. And not fun-size chocolate bars, either. The big ones. *Oh man.* "It's gonna be a long day," George muttered under his breath. "*Real* long."

"Okay, where should we go next?" Julianna asked after they had gone through George's dad's **obstacle course**; stopped, dropped, and rolled at Max's dad's firefighter booth; and flossed their teeth at Alex's mom's booth (even though George was embarrassed to see her again!).

But before the kids could decide what to do, Sage came running over in her bare feet.

"Where are your shoes?" George asked her.

"I've been helping out at my parents' yoga-studio booth," Sage explained. "You **don't wear shoes** when you do yoga."

George looked over to the corner

of the gym where Sage's parents were teaching yoga. A bunch of kids were standing on one leg and twisting their arms together like pretzels.

"I went to your dad's booth, *Georgie*," Sage assured him. "I signed my name really, really big on the sign-in sheet. Now you have to come try yoga at my parents' booth."

George **didn't really want** to do yoga. But it was only fair. "Okay," George said.

"I'll go, too," Alex agreed.

"Me three," Chris said.

"We'll all go," Julianna said.

Ruff! Ruff! Just then, the kids heard a dog barking.

"That's weird," Chris said. "Dogs aren't allowed in school. Not even for Career Day."

Ruff! Ruff!

"That's not a real dog," Sage said. "It's a recording. Mike's dad is demonstrating how he can identify the breed of a dog by its bark."

"Golden retriever," Mike's dad said.

"Right again, Dad," Mike told him. The kids at the booth all clapped.

"What does being a mailman have to do with dogs?" George wondered aloud.

"He says he's been **chased by so many dogs**, he can recognize them by their barks," Sage explained. "Mailmen really have to watch out for dogs."

Aarf. Aarf.

"Yorkshire terrier," Mike's dad guessed.

"Right again," Mike told his dad. "You're five for five."

The kids in the booth all cheered.

"Come on, Georgie," Sage said, pulling him by the elbow. "You're going to miss doing the eagle pose. It's my favorite."

To get to Sage's parents' booth, George had to pass Mr. Farley's station. Louie's dad was sitting behind a sign that read *Frederick Farley, Esquire.* A whole bunch of kids were sitting in chairs, listening to Louie's dad go on and on about being a lawyer. Well, not listening, really. Most of the kids were sleeping. One of them had **a little drool** coming out of the side of his mouth.

But that didn't matter. George and Louie hadn't bet that the kids at their dads' booths would have fun. They just bet that they would show up. And judging by how many kids were walking around the gym with **chocolate on their faces**, Louie had gotten a lot of people to come to his booth.

George looked down at his finger. It was such a cool ring. No one else in school had one like it. But it wasn't the idea of losing the ring that made George so sad. It was **losing it to Louie**. Because George could always get a new ring. But Louie would never let George forget that he'd lost the bet. And the only thing worse than being called Class Clown would be being called Loser to Louie.

Chapter 9

Huh?

As George and his friends walked toward Sage's parents' yoga station, Louie wheeled his way over to George and held out his hand.

George wasn't sure what to do. **Was this some sort of trick?** Did Louie want to shake his hand? And if he did, why?

Slowly, George put out his hand, too. Louie grabbed George's hand. But he didn't shake. Instead he turned it over and stared at **the skeleton ring**.

"I'm just making sure you're keeping my ring safe," Louie told George. "Mrs. Kelly said I had to leave my dad's booth and go to some other people's stations. But that's okay, because look how many people are listening to my dad right now."

George looked over. Louie was right. Lots more kids were eating chocolate at Mr. Farley's booth. He looked back to his dad's booth. There were a lot of kids there, too.

"You never know, Louie," George said. "Those sneakers might be mine."

"Oh, I do know," Louie said. "I know I'm going to win."

George didn't like the sound of that. It sounded like Louie had something sneaky up his sleeve—*again*. But what?

As Louie wheeled off on his sneakers, Sage took George's outstretched hand.

George yanked his hand away, fast.

But Sage just smiled and did that **weird eyelash-fluttering thing** she always did when she looked at George. "Come on, Georgie," she said. "Yoga will make you feel better."

But Sage was wrong. Yoga didn't make George feel better. It made him feel twisted and tangled and all tied up.

"Breathe in deeply and wrap your right leg over your left," Sage's mother said in a calm, gentle voice. "Now wrap your left arm over your right."

All the kids at the yoga-center booth wrapped their arms and legs tightly.

"Whoa!" George exclaimed as his body **wobbled back and forth** on his one standing leg.

"Breathe," Sage's mother reminded him.

Was she kidding? George was balancing on one leg, with his arms and legs twisted around each other, and she wanted him to breathe, too?

Besides, it was pretty hard to breathe

when there was something going on in
the bottom of your belly. Something **bing-
bonging**. And **zing-zonging**.

The super burp was back! And it didn't
feel like standing still on one leg. It felt like
bursting out!

But there was no way George was going
to let that happen! Not here. Not in the
middle of Career Day. He had to **squelch
that burp**.

But it wasn't going to be easy. The burp
had made a career of bursting out at the

worst possible times. Already the bubbles were ping-ponging on top of George's pancreas and ricocheting off his ribs.

There had to be a way to stop those bubbles. George had to confuse them so they didn't know which way was up and which way was down. It was the only way he could keep from burping.

So George started **hopping up and down** on his one leg that was still touching the ground. Up. Down. Up. Down.

The bubbles went up and down. Up to his throat, and then down to his kidneys. Then up to his bladder. Then down to his belly. Then . . .

POP! Suddenly George felt the air rush right out of him. Like someone had popped a balloon in the bottom of his belly. **The magic burp was gone.** George had squelched the belch!

"Whoa!" George was so excited he lost his balance and fell over—right into Alex.

"Whoops!" Alex cried out, as he slammed into Chris.

"Watch out!" Chris shouted as he tumbled into Julianna.

"Wheeee!" Juliana yelled as she plunged into Sage.

A minute later, the kids were all **lying on the floor** in a big heap. George opened his mouth to say, "I'm sorry." And that's exactly what came out.

"AAAHHHH! NO!" Suddenly a scream came from across the gym floor.

George turned around just in time to see Louie leaping up from the barber chair in the middle of Mr. Stubbs's barber-shop booth.

"Sorry, Louie," Mr. Stubbs said. "Thanks for volunteering to be my hair model. But **I can't cut your hair if you have lice**."

"I can't have lice," Louie insisted loudly. "Farleys don't get lice."

George watched as Mr. Farley walked over to where Louie was **having his fit**. Louie's dad was scratching at his head, too.

"Uh-oh," Mr. Stubbs told Louie's dad. "Looks like you and your son are going to have to go home and get deloused."

That was all anyone in the gym needed to hear. Suddenly, all the kids in Mr. Farley's booth leaped up from their seats. They couldn't get out of that booth fast enough.

A smile broke out across George's face. There was still an hour of Career Day left. Lots of kids were heading to his dad's station. And none of those kids would be going to Louie's dad's booth anymore. There was no one there to talk to them.

Now George knew he was going to **win the bet**.

Louie knew it, too. He walked over to George. "You cheated," he said angrily.

George was blown away. "*I* cheated?" he asked. "Are you kidding? I'm not the one who paid my friends to get people to come to my dad's booth. That was you. And you're the one who bribed people with chocolate."

"I didn't cheat—and you can't prove it, anyway. But you made sure you wouldn't get lice when I did," Louie insisted.

George didn't know what to say. How do you argue with something that doesn't even make sense?

"A bet's a bet," Louie told him grumpily. **"The wheelie sneakers are yours."**

George shook his head. "No thanks," he said.

"What?" Louie asked.

"What?" Mike and Max wondered.

"What?" Alex, Chris, Sage, and Julianna repeated.

"I don't want the sneakers," George said. "You keep them. I'm canceling the bet."

"Yeah, right," Louie huffed. "What's the catch?"

"No catch," George told him. **"The bet's off."**

Nurse Cuttaway left her health-care career booth and came over to talk to Louie. "I'm afraid you and your father will have to leave now," she told him. "We can't have people with lice in the school building."

As Louie walked away, Alex shot George a funny look. "You're letting him off the hook?" he asked.

George nodded. "Yeah. Who wants sneakers that smell like **Louie's sweaty feet** anyway?"

"Gotcha," Alex said with a laugh. "You want to go hear about architecture from Chris's dad now?"

"Sure," George agreed.

As he walked off with his friends,

George grinned. This day had turned out better than he ever thought it would. He'd won the bet *and* Louie had to leave school to be deloused. Tomorrow was going to be **a Louie-free day**!

In fact, only one thing could make this day better: a burp-buster booth at Career Day. Because George would love to meet a burp-buster—and the sooner, the better.

About the Author

Nancy Krulik is the author of more than 150 books for children and young adults including three *New York Times* Best Sellers and the popular Katie Kazoo, Switcheroo books. She lives in New York City with her family, and many of George Brown's escapades are based on things her own kids have done. (No one delivers a good burp quite like Nancy's son, Ian!) Nancy's favorite thing to do is laugh, which comes in pretty handy when you're trying to write funny books! You can follow Nancy on Twitter @NancyKrulik.

About the Illustrator

Aaron Blecha was raised by a school of giant squid in Wisconsin and now lives with his family by the south English seaside. He works as an artist designing funny characters and illustrating humorous books, including the one you're holding. You can enjoy more of his weird creations at www.monstersquid.com.